Ghost Rider:

The Final Journey on the Underground Railroad

by Steph DeFerie

Baker's Plays
7611 Sunset Blvd.
Los Angeles, CA 90042
BAKERSPLAYS.COM

GHOST RIDER was first staged by the Chatham Middle School Drama Club on Cape Cod, Massachusetts on May 12, 2007. The show was directed by Karen McPherson and stage managed by Ashley Shaffer and Rachael Weber. Sound was by Michael Sequin and lighting was by Patrick Corb. The cast was as follows:

MR. WILLIAMS	Tommy Rayder
MRS. WILLIAMS	Lily Kaar
JANIE	Sarah Lanning
TY	Liam Phelan
MAGGIE	Abigail Grattan
BECKA	Michaela Ryder
SUZE	Brianna Jarvis
MR. JAMESON	Damien Chandler
MRS. JAMESON	Kelsey Morse
FAITH	Courtney Milley
ELIJAH	Jonathan Morse
TEMPERANCE	Susan Hart
SLATTERY	Kyle Forgeron
COOMBS	Griffin McLain
MADAME ROSA	Ella Nichols
REVEREND MATTHEWS	Jonas Greenblatt
MRS. COLLINS	Rachel Jerauld
CALICO	Indie Fleuriot
FAST	Cooper Seidewant
SLOW	Lucas Parada
PROFESSOR PORTERFOY	Patti DeTraglia
NEIGHBORHOOD GIRLS	Mackenzie Barnard Connie LaMott

CHARACTERS

Present Day:

MR. WILLIAMS
MRS. WILLIAMS
MAGGIE – their daughter
TY – their son
JANIE – their daughter
SUZE – a neighbor girl
BECKA – a neighbor girl
MADAME ROSA – a psychic
PROFESSOR POTRTERFOY – a historian

1855:

MR. JAMESON
MRS. JAMESON
ELIJAH – their son
TEMPERANCE – their daughter
FAITH – their daughter
REVEREND MATTHEWS
CALICO – a runaway slave
FAST – a runaway slave
SLOW – a runaway slave
MR. COLLINS – a conductor
SLATTERY – a slave hunter
COOMBS – a slave hunter

TIME

Today & 1855

PLACE

The living room of a house in Ohio

Act 1 Scene 1 – Present Day
Act 1 Scene 2 – 1855
Act 1 Scene 3 – Present Day, a few days later
Act 1 Scene 4 – 1855, a few days later
Act 2 – Present Day, three days later

For my ghosts - Gram, Pop, Nunu and especially Jack.

ACT ONE

Scene One

(The living room of a house in Ohio. It's a large room with a door to the outside and a doorway to the kitchen and rest of the house. There is a large window and a fireplace and a bookcase that is actually a door with a little secret room behind it. There is the usual furniture – couch, chairs, tables. The furniture is nondescript and colonial. The light is provided by a chandelier that hangs over the center of the room – the light bulbs are in the shape of candle flames – and the window.)

*(**AT RISE:** It is today. The room is gloomy, lit only by light that comes in through the dirty window. The furniture is covered by sheets. There is some debris and trash. Some of the furniture has been knocked over.)*

(Silence. Emptiness. Abandonment. Stillness.)

(Suddenly, an indistinct shadow flits across. There is a soft, sorrowful cry. The chandelier sways. We hear a few notes from the old song "Follow The Drinking Gourd." Something falls from the bookcase shelves. Silence and stillness again.)

*(Enter through the front door the Williams family – **MR. WILLIAMS, MRS. WILLIAMS, MAGGIE, TY** and **JANIE**. **MAGGIE** is clutching a Barbie doll. They are carrying suitcases, boxes, bags. They turn on the lights, take off the cloths, exit and re-enter with more things, exit to explore the house and put away things, place books and knick-knacks on the bookcase shelves, unpack a bit, etc.)*

MR. WILLIAMS. Well, here it is! Our new home! What do you think?

MRS. WILLIAMS. It stinks! (**MR. WILLIAMS** *gives her a look.*) No, really! What is that smell? *(She sniffs.)* Are raccoons living here? Wet raccoons?

MR. WILLIAMS. It just needs a little cleaning up is all. *(At the window)* Look at that view!

MAGGIE. Mommy, it smells in here! P-ew!

MAGGIE, JANIE, TY, MRS. WILLIAMS. P-ew! P-ew!

(**MR. WILLIAMS** *gives them a look. The* **CHILDREN** *stop.* **MRS. WILLIAMS** *continues:*)

MRS. WILLIAMS. P-ew! P… *(She trails off.)*

MR. WILLIAMS. You children are a very bad influence on your mother.

TY. How's the yard?

(**TY** *exits out front door.*)

MR. WILLIAMS. It'll be fine once we air it out, you'll see. It's just a little moldy is all.

MRS. WILLIAMS. A *little* moldy? It's a mushroom farm in here. Bring in some pigs and we'll search for truffles.

MAGGIE. What are truffles, Mommy?

MRS. WILLIAMS. Over-priced fungus.

JANIE. There's a fungus among us!

MRS. WILLIAMS. You can say that again.

JANIE & MAGGIE. A fungus among us! A fungus among us!

MRS. WILLIAMS. I don't seem to recall it being quite this bad when the realtor showed it to us.

MAGGIE. Are we bringing in pigs to live with us, Mommy? The three little pigs?

MRS. WILLIAMS. No, dear. No self-respecting pig would leave his clean, little sty for this place.

MR. WILLIAMS. Look at these classic lines! It's a piece of history.

MRS. WILLIAMS. It's a piece of something, all right.

JANIE. Oh, Daddy. You're always going on about history. It's sooooo boring. It never has anything to do with anything.

(**JANIE** *exits to kitchen.*)

MR. WILLIAMS. (*Calling after her*) It has everything to do everything. You children never listen to me. Think of the stories this place could tell. It was built in the early 1800's, for God's sake.

MRS. WILLIAMS. And I don't think anyone's dusted since. Let's hope the plumbing at least is from the 20th century. I am not an outhouse kind of girl.

MAGGIE. What's an outhouse, Mommy?

MRS. WILLIAMS. A place where you pee outside.

MAGGIE. Yuck! I'm not going to pee outside.

MRS. WILLIAMS. Neither am I.

MR. WILLIAMS. They really built 'em to last back then.

(**MR. WILLIAMS** *slams his hand against the bookcase and one of the shelves falls down.*)

MR. WILLIAMS. Oops! And don't even get me started on the price. It's a steal!

MRS. WILLIAMS. Somebody certainly stole from somebody, that's for sure. (*Seeing* **MR. WILLIAMS**' *disappointed look*) I suppose it does have…possibilities.

MAGGIE. (*Pointing up to a corner*) Are those possibilities, Mommy?

MRS. WILLIAMS. No, dear, those are cobwebs.

TY. (*Entering*) Dad, you should see this great tree out back! It's perfect for a tree house!

MR. WILLIAMS. Ty, do you think the tree house could wait a few minutes while we get all this stuff inside? (*Looking at his watch*) We made good time. The movers won't be here for an hour.

MRS. WILLIAMS. That gives you plenty of time to get organized while I go pick up some groceries.

(**JANIE** *enters humming "Follow The Drinking Gourd."* **MRS. WILLIAMS** *exits to kitchen.*)

JANIE. I call the big bedroom in the back.

TY. No fair! I haven't gotten to see it yet!

(*TY exits to kitchen.*)

MR. WILLIAMS. Ty!

JANIE. It is so fair. I called it.

MR. WILLIAMS. Actually, Janie, I think that bedroom's already spoken for.

JANIE. If I have to share with Maggie, we need the biggest one.

MR. WILLIAMS. Your mother and I have to share, too, you know.

JANIE. That doesn't count. You don't need so much room because you two sleep in the same bed.

MRS. WILLIAMS. *(O.S.)* Not when someone's had chili for dinner we don't.

JANIE. And anyway, you didn't call it.

(**MRS. WILLIAMS** *enters, humming a few notes from* "Follow The Drinking Gourd.")

MR. WILLIAMS. I don't have to call it – I'm the father.

JANIE. *Everybody* has to call it. That's the rules.

(**JANIE** *picks up a box of toys and exits to kitchen.*)

MRS. WILLIAMS. She's got you, you know. That is the rules.

MR. WILLIAMS. *(Calling after)* That's our room, young lady! Don't put your stuff in there because you'll just have to move it all back out again! *(To* **MRS. WILLIAMS***)* She gets pigheadedness from your side of the family, you know. *(Sniffs)* Remember to pick up some air freshener.

(**MR. WILLIAMS** *exits outside.*)

MAGGIE. P-ew! P-ew!

MRS. WILLIAMS. Honey, please. Do you want to come with Mommy to the store and pick out something for dinner?

MAGGIE. Waffles!

MRS. WILLIAMS. That's what we had for breakfast.

MAGGIE. Waffles!

MRS. WILLIAMS. Is that all you can say?

MAGGIE & MRS. WILLIAMS. Waffles!

MRS. WILLIAMS. What do you have in your head instead of brains?

MAGGIE and **MRS. WILLIAMS.** Waffles!

(**TY** *and* **JANIE** *enter.* **TY** *is now humming some of the song.*)

JANIE. My bedroom, my bedroom, my bedroom!

TY. Keep your old bedroom, I don't care. I'm going to live up in the attic. It's cool up there.

JANIE. Aren't you afraid of ghosts? They live in attics, you know, with the bats and the monsters.

TY. I'm not afraid of ghosts. There's no such things as ghosts.

JANIE. There are, too!

TY. Are not!

JANIE. Are, too! My friend Patty saw one.

TY. Oh, yeah? Where?

JANIE. In her grandmother's closet. It was wearing her grandmother's dress and her grandmother's big, floppy hat and it went "Whhhhooooo, whoooooo!"

TY. Aw, she's making that up.

(**JANIE** *exits to kitchen.*)

MAGGIE. Mommy, I don't want to live in a house with ghosty closets.

MRS. WILLIAMS. There are no ghosty closets here, honey. Janie, stop scaring your sister.

(**MR. WILLIAMS** *enters carrying boxes. He is now humming the song.*)

MAGGIE. Daddy, are there ghosts?

MR. WILLIAMS. If there are, I sure wish they'd come and give me a hand.

TY. Dad, can I have my room up in the attic?

MR. WILLIAMS. You can have anything you want if you help bring in all these boxes from the trailer.

TY. Anything? Really? How about a monster truck?

(**JANIE** *enters.*)

JANIE. If Ty's getting a monster truck, I want a monster truck. Mommy, there's something all gross in the oven. I think it's a dead poisoned dog!

TY. I wanna see!

MAGGIE. Me, too!

(*TY and MAGGIE rush off to kitchen.*)

MR. WILLIAMS. Ty!

JANIE. I'm not eating anything that comes out of that oven, I can tell you that.

(*JANIE picks up another box and exits to kitchen.*)

MAGGIE. (*Entering*) Gross! We're having dead poisoned dogs for dinner!

MR. WILLIAMS. Ty! Get back here!

MRS. WILLIAMS. We are most certainly not having dead poisoned dogs for dinner.

MR. WILLIAMS. We will if you don't get moving.

MRS. WILLIAMS. We're going. Come one, Magpie.

(*MRS. WILLIAMS grabs MAGGIE and pulls her with her. As she passes MR. WILLIAMS, she grabs a kiss.*)

MRS. WILLIAMS. What's that song you're humming?

MR. WILLIAMS. How should I know? I picked it up from you.

(*MRS. WILLIAMS and MAGGIE exit out front door, leaving it open. BECKA and SUZE, neighbor children, poke their heads in.*)

MR. WILLIAMS. Kids! Leave the dead, poisoned dog in the oven alone and come help me! (*He notices the girls.*) There really isn't a dead, poisoned dog in the oven, you know. It just looks that way. (*They stare at him in astonishment*). Who are you?

BECKA. I'm Becka.

SUZE. I'm Suze. (*She gestures vaguely.*) We live over there.

BECKA. We came to see who would live in a haunted house.

MR. WILLIAMS. What makes you think this house is haunted?

(Enter TY, *covered in a sheet and chasing* JANIE.*)*

TY. I'm the ghost of the dead, poisoned dog!

JANIE. Daddy! Make him stop!

TY. Why did you poison me?!

JANIE. Daddy!

MR. WILLIAMS. *(To* BECKA *and* SUZE*)* You see? Not a ghost in sight. Becka, Suze, these are the children I adopted who are going right back to the orphanage if they don't start helping.

SUZE. Really?

MR. WILLIAMS. They'll have to toil from dawn to dusk braiding hair extensions for wealthy Chinese opium lords and eating gruel and cockroach sandwiches.

BECKA. They will?

MR. WILLIAMS. They will if they don't get their butts in gear.

*(*MR. WILLIAMS *exits outside.)*

SUZE. Gosh! That sounds even worse than living in a haunted house.

BECKA. Nothing's worse than living in a haunted house.

JANIE. Who's living in a haunted house?

BECKA. You are.

JANIE. We are not.

SUZE. You are too. Everybody knows this place is haunted.

TY. Of course it is, that's why we bought it. We looked all over the world for the most haunted house of all and this is it.

JANIE. Yeah, it's cool to live in a haunted house.

BECKA. I bet you won't say that when the ghosts get you.

JANIE. We eat dead poisoned dogs for dinner. Ghosts don't scare us.

TY. Just what kind of ghosts live here exactly?

SUZE. A kid who got eaten!

TY. Really? Cool!

BECKA. You see, a long time ago...

SUZE. Hundreds and hundreds of years ago…

BECKA. There was this family that lived here…

> *(A light change. We are seeing the* **JAMESON** *family who lived in the house in 1855. Because they are in the past, they do not see or interact with the children. Likewise, the children can neither see nor hear the Jamesons.)*

> *(Enter* **MR. JAMESON** *through front door, carrying a load of logs that he begins to stack by the fireplace.)*

MR. JAMESON. Mother, it's me!

MRS. JAMESON. *(O.S.)* Thomas? What are you doing home so early?

MR. JAMESON. Hiram had already cut and sized the planks so we just had to nail them together. I felt guilty about taking the firewood he promised for such little work but he insisted. He's a good man, Hiram.

MRS. JAMESON. *(Entering with a mug of coffee that she gives to* **MR. JAMESON***)* He sides with the abolitionists, you know. Have you had your dinner?

MR. JAMESON. No, I didn't want to take the time.

MRS. JAMESON. Goodness, I didn't know I had such charms to draw you back in such a hurry.

MR. JAMESON. *(He kisses her.)* I do believe you are one of the fabled sirens in that old story. Well, what if he does side with the abolitionists? So do I.

MRS. JAMESON. But he puts his words into actions.

MR. JAMESON. He has no children to endanger if he is caught.

BECKA. A mom and dad and three kids…

> *(Enter* **FAITH, ELIJAH** *and* **TEMPERANCE** *who carries a doll.)*

TEMPERANCE, FAITH, ELIJAH. Papa!

ELIJAH. You were supposed to be gone all day!

MR. JAMESON. We finished early and I knew how much you wanted to start your tree house…

ELIJAH. Now?

MR. JAMESON. Have you done your chores?

ELIJAH. Every one.

MR. JAMESON. Then let the construction begin!

ELIJAH. Hooray!

TEMPERANCE. Hello, Papa.

FAITH. We missed you at prayers last night.

MR. JAMESON. *(Teasing)* You missed me choosing a short passage, you mean. I'm sure Mama had you on your poor, sore knees for hours.

FAITH. Hours and hours and hours!

TEMPERANCE. I almost fainted it was so long! Miss Alice swooned!

MRS. JAMESON. Yes, that's me – the mean, old mother who will push, pull or drag her children into the kingdom of Heaven by any means necessary.

FAITH. Even if we have to travel through Hell to get there?

MR. & MRS. JAMESON. *(Shocked)* Faith!

BECKA. They were mean and horrible to their kids…

MR. JAMESON. I'm surprised at you!

SUZE. They made them work day and night and only gave them scraps of bread to eat and rags to wear and made them sleep out in the barn where they almost froze to death every single night…

MRS. JAMESON. I should wash your mouth out with soap for saying such a thing!

FAITH. For telling the truth?

MR. JAMESON. Kneeling at prayer a few minutes every night can scarcely compare to the torments of Hell.

FAITH. It can to me.

MR. JAMESON. *(With mock seriousness)* With that attitude, young lady, you don't deserve the present I brought you. I shall give it to some more deserving child instead.

TEMPERANCE. I'm deserving, Papa!

MR. JAMESON. Deserving but greedy! All the presents shall go to the Sutter children down the road.

TEMPERANCE & FAITH & ELIJAH. Papa!

MRS. JAMESON. *(Teasing)* You are very wise, Thomas. They are much more worthy of them.

TEMPERANCE & FAITH & ELIJAH. Noooo!

MR. JAMESON. I'll go take them right away...

TEMPERANCE & FAITH & ELIJAH. Papa, no! Please! We'll be good, honest! *(etc)*

(The **JAMESONS** *all exit out the front door. The lights change back.)*

BECKA. ...and finally they ran away and the parents realized they needed someone to do all the work so they caught an orphan but he wouldn't do what they said so they pushed him into the oven and cooked him and ate him!

TY. Aw, get out! That's "Hansel and Gretel."

SUZE. It is not. That's not a dead, poisoned dog in the oven – it's the kid!

BECKA. And his ghost still haunts here to this very day. He can't rest or anything. He wanders around moaning and crying and looking for somebody to eat.

(**MR. WILLIAMS** *enters.)*

TY. Dad, these girls say that the people who used to live here once killed a kid and ate him.

MR. WILLIAMS. So that's why we got it so cheap. Well, we can't afford to leave now so I hope you're all very brave.

(There's the sound of knocking.)

MR. WILLIAMS. It's open!

JANIE. That's not the door, Daddy. It's coming from the kitchen. It's the ghost!

TY. It's the dead poisoned dog trying to get out of the oven!

MR. WILLIAMS. Your mother must have forgotten something and come back, that's all.

TY. In the kitchen? Why didn't she use the front door?

SUZE. It *is* the ghost!

MR. WILLIAMS. It's not a ghost! It's air in the pipes. It happens all the time in old houses like this.

(**MR. WILLIAMS** *starts to exit.*)

JANIE. Daddy, don't go in there!

MR. WILLIAMS. *(Scary voice)* If I'm not out in 10 seconds, run for your lives.

(**MR. WILLIAMS** *exits to the kitchen.*)

TY. Dad, wait!

JANIE. Come back!

BECKA. *(Whispering)* Too bad the ghost is gonna get him – he looked like a nice dad.

(*There is a long silence. Suddenly…*)

MR. WILLIAMS. *(Screaming off)* No! Help! Don't eat me! Help! Help!

TY & JANIE. Daddy!

(*The **KIDS** rush for the door to the kitchen. The front door opens and **MRS. WILLIAMS** and **MAGGIE** enter.*)

MRS. WILLIAMS. What's all the screaming for? Has anyone seen… ?

TY & JANIE. The ghost has Daddy!

MRS. WILLIAMS. What?

JANIE. The ghost of the dead poisoned dog!

SUZE. The ghost of the kid who got eaten!

JANIE. He's going to eat Daddy!

TY. It's in the kitchen!

JANIE. We have to save him!

(**MR. WILLIAMS** *sticks his head in from the kitchen.*)

MR. WILLIAMS. *(Smiling)* Got ya!

(*The **KIDS** and **MRS. WILLIAMS** scream. **MR. WILLIAMS** screams.*)

MRS. WILLIAMS. What is going on in here?!

Blackout

Scene Two

(1855.)

(All traces of the modern scene have been removed – boxes, bags, cloths on the furniture, people, etc. The room is quite set up. Enter **MR. JAMESON** *and* **MRS. JAMESON**.*)*

MRS. JAMESON. …and the poor man was on the bank of the river, his freedom just on the other side, when those horrible slave catchers grabbed him and returned him to bondage again.

MR. JAMESON. It is terrible. It is the most terrible thing I have ever heard. But there is nothing I can do!

MRS. JAMESON. There is!

MR. JAMESON. At what cost? You would have me endanger our children for the lives of strangers? What good am I to this family if I am in prison?

MRS. JAMESON. What good are you to this family if you do not have the courage to act on your principles?

MR. JAMESON. Principles are all very well but they do not provide for a roof overhead and food in the belly.

MRS. JAMESON. It is just as important to provide the example of courage.

MR. JAMESON. That is easy to say now when you are far from danger.

MRS. JAMESON. This life matters nothing compared to the everlasting life with our Lord. Whatever we lose here shall be returned to us a hundred fold if it is lost in a just cause.

MR. JAMESON. But that does not mean we should throw away so lightly what we do have. Our children depend on me.

MRS. JAMESON. And who is to say we shall be caught? People, good people, help escaping slaves every day and are never found out.

(A knock at the front door. **MR. JAMESON** *crosses and opens it.)*

MR. JAMESON. Can I help you?

SLATTERY. *(Pushing* **MR. JAMESON** *aside and entering carrying a rifle)* Stand aside! We're here to enforce the Fugitive Slave Act!

COOMBS. *(Entering, carrying a rifle)* Move away, there.

MR. JAMESON. Who are you?

SLATTERY. Slattery. *(He indicates* **COOMBS.***)* Coombs.

MR. JAMESON. How dare you barge… !

SLATTERY. We have reason to believe you are harboring runaway slaves.

COOMBS. Breaking the law, you are.

MR. JAMESON. You have no right to come into my home.

COOMBS. Oh, we have the right.

SLATTERY. We have every right as good citizens who want to see the law upheld.

MR. JAMESON. Are you federal marshals, then?

MRS. JAMESON. Of course they are not! Look at them. They are filthy bounty hunters. Get out!

SLATTERY. It makes no difference if we are marshals or not.

COOMBS. No difference at all.

SLATTERY. You are required to help us.

MRS. JAMESON. We will not help you.

COOMBS. I think they're obstructing justice, Slats.

SLATTERY. Are you refusing to aid us in our search?

MRS. JAMESON. With all the strength God gives me. You do the devil's work.

SLATTERY. We do the work of the law.

COOMBS. The law, missus.

MRS. JAMESON. Man's law, not God's.

COOMBS. The Slave Act requires that you help us.

SLATTERY. If you refuse, you'll be arrested on charges of obstruction.

MR. JAMESON. No law may compel me to help you. Although I have never aided runaway slaves, I will never aid those who seek to capture them and return them to slavery.

SLATTERY. The law is the law.

MRS. JAMESON. The law is wrong!

SLATTERY. That is not for you to say. It is for you to obey.

COOMBS. To obey!

MRS. JAMESON. The government should not force us to do what we feel is morally unjust.

SLATTERY. I don't have time to debate a law that is already on the books.

COOMBS. Move aside!

(**SLATTERY** *and* **COOMBS** *begin to ransack the room, looking for evidence.*)

MRS. JAMESON. What makes you think we are helping slaves?

SLATTERY. We know a farm in this area is acting as a refuge.

MRS. JAMESON. So you have no proof that we are the ones you are looking for.

SLATTERY. We're searching everyone.

COOMBS. All the farms around here.

MR. JAMESON. Then it is you who act in defiance of the law. You must have some proof to search us. You cannot come in here without good evidence. If you do not leave immediately, I shall have *you* arrested.

(**SLATTERY** *and* **COOMBS** *look unsure.*)

MRS. JAMESON. Now go!

(**SLATTERY** *and* **COOMBS** *begin to cross to the front door.*)

SLATTERY. We'll go but we'll be watching you!

COOMBS. We ain't finished with you yet.

(**SLATTERY** *and* **COOMBS** *exit through front door.*)

MRS. JAMESON. There! You see! How can you stand by and let that happen?

MR. JAMESON. (*Shaken, closing the door*) That is not right. By God, that is not right!

MRS. JAMESON. What are you going to do about it?

MR. JAMESON. I must think upon it and weigh the consequences.

MRS. JAMESON. Listen to what God moves your heart to…

(Enter through the kitchen doorway **ELIJAH**, **FAITH** *and* **TEMPERANCE** *who carries her doll.)*

ELIJAH, FAITH, TEMPERANCE. Papa! Mama!

MRS. JAMESON. Where have you been? You must leave those new kittens alone. Your chores…

TEMPERANCE. We saw it, we saw it with our own eyes! In town… !

FAITH. It was terrible! The children were crying and crying!

ELIJAH. They were just like us… !

TEMPERANCE. …except they were brown instead of white…

ELIJAH. …and they were being dragged away in chains!.

MRS. JAMESON. What are you talking about?

FAITH. They were slave children and we saw them captured!

ELIJAH. They were taken away from their Mama and no one did anything to stop it!

TEMPERANCE. It was the most terrible thing I've ever seen in my whole life! No one will ever take us away from you, Mama, will they?

MRS. JAMESON. Of course not, dearest. You're perfectly safe. *(With a look to* **MR. JAMESON***)* God has blessed us with white skin and you must be thankful of that every day.

ELIJAH. I'd fight them if they tried to take me away. They'd be sorry they came for me.

FAITH. You couldn't fight those big men. They'd put chains on you and drag you off just like those others.

ELIJAH. They didn't even try to fight or get away. Why didn't they, Papa?

MR. JAMESON. I don't know, Elijah. Maybe they were tired of running and just gave up.

MRS. JAMESON. Maybe they knew no one would help them so there wasn't any use in fighting.

ELIJAH. You would've helped them if you'd been there, wouldn't you, Papa?

TEMPERANCE. Of course he would've. He would've beaten those mean, old slave catchers until they let them go. Right, Papa?

MR. JAMESON. Children, sometimes things are not as simple as they…

FAITH. Then we could've brought them here and helped them escape.

ELIJAH. We could build them a secret room to hide in and Papa could take them in his wagon up to freedom in Canada.

FAITH. We could show them the kittens!

TEMPERANCE. *(Holding up her doll)* And they could play with Miss Alice if they liked. I wouldn't mind. When are they coming?

MR. JAMESON. There aren't any slaves coming here.

ELIJAH. Of course not, not until we build the secret room. It's not safe. *(He crosses to the bookcase.)* We could put it behind here, Papa, and build a false wall up in the kitchen to hide it.

FAITH. And they could use the quilt I'm making to keep warm!

TEMPERANCE. Miss Alice will have a tea party for them!

MR. JAMESON. We're doing no such thing! I'm very proud of you for wanting to help but it's very, very dangerous. It's not something for children to play at.

FAITH. But it wouldn't be just us. You'd have to help, too.

MR. JAMESON. It's out of the question. We are not going to aid runaway slaves.

FAITH. But we have to, Papa. Reverend Matthews was talking about it in church last week, remember?

TEMPERANCE. He said it's what Jesus would do. Don't you

want to be like Jesus?

MR. JAMESON. It's not as simple as that…

TEMPERANCE. Why not?

MR. JAMESON. Would you like to see your poor, old Papa go to jail for years and years if we were caught? All alone in a tiny cell with no fire to keep me warm?

TEMPERANCE. Poor Papa.

ELIJAH. But you wouldn't get caught, Papa. You're much too clever. *(To* **TEMPERANCE** *and* **FAITH***)* Come on, let's go start working on it.

FAITH. I'll be the runaway slave and you try to catch me.

TEMPERANCE. *(Giving doll to* **MR. JAMESON***)* You can take Miss Alice with you to prison, Papa, to keep you company. I won't mind.

*(***TEMPERANCE***, ***FAITH*** and ***ELIJAH*** exit to the kitchen.)*

MRS. JAMESON. Well, then, I guess it's settled.

MR. JAMESON. Don't be ridiculous. By tomorrow, they'll have forgotten all about it and be playing at Settlers and Indians.

MRS. JAMESON. Don't you want to be like Jesus?

MR. JAMESON. Now don't you start, Mother, you know this is not a game.

MRS. JAMESON. No, it's not. It is life and death to the slaves we could help.

MR. JAMESON. Bondage is not death.

MRS. JAMESON. Tell that to the children taken from their mother, children just like your own.

*(***MRS. JAMESON*** exits to kitchen.)*

MR. JAMESON. *(Looking at Miss Alice)* Children just like my own…

Blackout

Scene Three

(Today, a few days later.)

(The room is dark – the drapes are shut. The lights are low. **TY**, **JANIE**, **MAGGIE**, **SUZE** *and* **BECKA** *are sitting in a group on the floor or at a table using a Ouija board.)*

SUZE. Ghost of this house, come to us!

BECKA. Ghost of this house, speak to us!

TY. Ghost of this house, this is stupid!

JANIE. If you think it's so stupid, what are you doing it for?

TY. To prove to you how stupid it is. We're not going to get a message from beyond.

JANIE. That's what you think.

BECKA. Ghost, tell us what you want. What will appease your anger?

MAGGIE. Janie, I'm scared!

JANIE. It's all right. We're just going find out what the ghost wants so we can give it to him and he'll go away.

TY. What if what he wants is to eat somebody?

JANIE. Then we'll give him you!

SUZE. Give us a message, ghost!

(A book falls out of the bookcase.)

MAGGIE. Janie!

JANIE. It's the ghost, all right! He keeps doing that! *(To* **TY***)* See?

TY. What do you want? Tell us what you want!

(A pause.)

MR. WILLIAMS. *(Off, in a spooky voice)* I want…I want…baloney sandwiches for lunch!

(All the **KIDS** *jump in surprise.)*

*(**MR. WILLIAMS** enters from the kitchen, turning on the lights and opening the curtains.)*

JANIE. Daddy!

MR. WILLIAMS. You better not let your mother catch you doing this. You know she doesn't like you getting yourselves all worked up.

MAGGIE. *(Indicating* **SUZE** *and* **BECKA***)* They made us!

SUZE. Sorry, Mr. Williams. We thought if we could just make contact with the ghost we could ask him to leave.

MR. WILLIAMS. I know it's fun pretending there's a ghost, but Maggie's having bad dreams and it's upsetting your mother. Maybe you should stop playing for a while.

JANIE. We're not playing, Daddy. It's real.

MR. WILLIAMS. Now you know that's not true.

TY. Somebody pushed another book out of the bookcase.

MR. WILLIAMS. *(Re-shelving the book)* That's not ghosts.

JANIE. Then what is it? Books just don't jump down from their shelves, you know.

BECKA. And how do you explain that knocking?

MR. WILLIAMS. I told you, it's the plumbing. Air gets in the pipes…

SUZE. More like ghosts get in the pipes…

MR. WILLIAMS. Mice in the walls…

MAGGIE. Giant mice? That's even scarier than a ghost!

MR. WILLIAMS. There isn't any ghost!

*(***MRS. WILLIAMS*** enters from the front door.)*

MRS. WILLIAMS. I found someone to get rid of the ghost.

MR. WILLIAMS. You see? *(Does a double take)* What?

MRS. WILLIAMS. I've found someone to get rid of the ghost. A ghost buster.

MR. WILLIAMS. What is the woman I married who doesn't believe in ghosts?

MRS. WILLIAMS. *(Quietly)* If you can't beat 'em…Kids, run and get washed up for lunch. We're having company.

MAGGIE. Who is it, Mommy?

MRS. WILLIAMS. It's a surprise.

(The **KIDS** *exit.)*

MR. WILLIAMS. I'm assuming you have some kind of secret plan and haven't just lost your mind.

MRS. WILLIAMS. Look, they're all convinced this place is haunted whether we say it is or not, right? We're never going to have a moment's peace until we persuade them that it isn't. So I'm going to have an expert clear out the ghost and we're all set.

MR. WILLIAMS. And you found this expert in the yellow pages under "Crazy Pants?"

MRS. WILLIAMS. Mrs. Bishop down at the drugstore told me about Madame Rosa…

MR. WILLIAMS. Aaahh, Mrs. Bishop, I should have known! And who, pray tell, is Madame Rosa?

MRS. WILLIAMS. The local soothsayer. No matter what your problem, Madame's got a spell or a charm or a potion.

MR. WILLIAMS. And she can help us…how?

MRS. WILLIAMS. She's also…psychic.

MR. WILLIAMS. Oooohh!

MRS. WILLIAMS. I dropped in to see her this morning, crossed her palm with silver and she's making a house call this afternoon.

MR. WILLIAMS. I had no idea you were so devious. It's wonderful.

MRS. WILLIAMS. She is going to come in, read the vibrations, make contact with the lingering shade and purge him from our lives once and for all.

MR. WILLIAMS. I will never underestimate you again.

MRS. WILLIAMS. I should hope not. This is all your fault, you know. If you hadn't encouraged them to begin with…

MR. WILLIAMS. I didn't think they would take it so seriously.

MRS. WILLIAMS. She promised to put on a good show and things will get back to normal.

MAGGIE. *(O.S.)* Mommy! Janie's splashing me!

JANIE. *(O.S.)* I am not! Ty's splashing me!

MRS. WILLIAMS. Well, just splash him back then!

(**MRS. WILLIAMS** *exits to kitchen.*)

MR. WILLIAMS. *(Singing and dancing around a bit)* "Who you gonna call? Ghostbusters!"

(**MR. WILLIAMS** *dances by the bookcase and another book falls out.* **MR. WILLIAMS** *jumps back, surprised and a bit scared.*)

(*A knock at the front door.* **MR. WILLIAMS** *jumps again and then crosses to answer it.*)

MR. WILLIAMS. *(Opening door)* Hello, can I help you?

MADAME ROSA. Oh, I believe it is *I* who can help *you*. I am… Madame Rosa.

MR. WILLIAMS. Wonderful! I'm…

MADAME ROSA. Don't tell me! You are…*(She puts her hands to her head.)*…the butler!

MR. WILLIAMS. I'm Mr. Williams.

MADAME ROSA. And since you just answered the door, there for a moment, you were, in fact, the butler.

MR. WILLIAMS. Well, if you want to look at it that way…

MADAME ROSA. Ta da! My psychic powers are truly amazing!

MR. WILLIAMS. Okay. Won't you come in?

MADAME ROSA. Wait! I must prepare myself. *(She does. Entering)* Doom! Despair! Evil! I sense the presence of great, overpowering, black evil! Oh, what a charming room! You've fixed it up wonderfully. *(Notices* **MR. WILLIAMS** *is staring at her)* Please don't be intimidated by my awesome powers. In many ways, I'm just like you. Treat me exactly as you would any normal person.

MR. WILLIAMS. I'll try. *(Calling)* Honey, your special guest is here.

MADAME ROSA. I'm afraid I'm a bit early but I had a very strong feeling that you needed me right away.

MR. WILLIAMS. That's very crazy of…uh, *thoughtful* of you.

(**MRS. WILLIAMS** *enters from kitchen.*)

MRS. WILLIAMS. Who's crazy?

MR. WILLIAMS. No one. Not one crazy person as far as the eye can see.

MRS. WILLIAMS. Madame Rosa! Thank you so much for coming.

MADAME ROSA. It's a good thing you called me when you did. The moment I walked in, I could sense the malevolent spirit that inhabits this house.

(**MADAME ROSA** *looks pointedly at* **MR. WILLIAMS.**)

MR. WILLIAMS. What'd I do?

MRS. WILLIAMS. *(Calling)* Kids! The surprise is here!

(The **KIDS** *enter.)*

TY. Is it my monster truck?

JANIE. Is it *my* monster truck?

MRS. WILLIAMS. It's Madame Rosa. *(The* **KIDS** *look disappointed.)* She is not a monster truck but you're going to be very happy she's here. Madame Rosa, these are my children Ty, Janie and Maggie and these are their friends Becka and Suze

MADAME ROSA. Children are very sensitive, you know. I myself was quite touched as a child.

MR. WILLIAMS. I don't doubt that for a minute.

MRS. WILLIAMS. *(With a black look at* **MR. WILLIAMS**) Yes, they're the ones who first noticed that something was wrong.

MADAME ROSA. I see. And exactly what sort of manifestations are you experiencing?

JANIE. What?

MADAME ROSA. What's going on?

TY. Something keeps knocking in this wall.

JANIE. And books jump out of the bookcase.

SUZE. It's always cold in here.

BECKA. And there was a poisoned, dead dog in the oven.

MAGGIE. *(Whispering loudly)* Mommy doesn't believe us. Daddy says he does but he doesn't really.

JANIE. And we all keep humming the same stupid song.

MADAME ROSA. What song?

> *(EVERYONE but* **MADAME ROSA** *hums "Follow The Drinking Gourd.")*

SUZE. And don't forget the crying.

MRS. WILLIAMS. What crying?

BECKA. We heard somebody crying this morning.

TY. That doesn't count – it was just Maggie because she couldn't find her stupid Barbie doll.

MAGGIE. It was not me! And you give me back my Barbie, Tyler! I know you took her!

TY. I did not! Dad, I didn't… !

BECKA. So crying *and* doll-stealing.

MRS. WILLIAMS. That Barbie gets lost and found ten times before breakfast. I don't think that really counts.

TY. What do you want to know for?

MADAME ROSA. Because I am a psychic, my dear boy. I am in touch with the spirits who have passed on from this realm and have not yet moved on to the next.

JANIE. Like that man we saw on TV. Daddy said he was a big fat fake who fooled people and took their money.

MR. WILLIAMS. *(Uncomfortable)* Well, yes…*he* was a fake. But you, Madame Rosa, anybody can tell that you are the real thing.

MADAME ROSA. *(Icily)* It is very difficult to work with unbelievers in the room. Their negative vibrations quite interfere with my sensitivity.

MRS. WILLIAMS. Of course. We totally understand. Would we have invited you here if we thought you were less than gifted?

MADAME ROSA. I suppose not.

TY. Can you see the ghost flying around the room right now?

MADAME ROSA. *(To* **MR. WILLIAMS***)* I can *feel* distressing currents of energy flowing among us.

MAGGIE. *(Brushing wildly at her hair)* It is in my hair?!

MADAME ROSA. It is all around us, my dear, but do not fear. It cannot harm you. I am going to try to make contact with it and persuade it to move on.

BECKA. Move far, far on because we live just over there and we don't want it moving into *our* house.

MADAME ROSA. Let us begin.

> (**MADAME ROSA** *sweeps around the room very dramatically, waving her hands around to feel the vibrations, following the movements of invisible beings only she can see, etc. She ends up as far from the bookcase as possible.*)

MADAME ROSA. Yes, yes, the energy is very strong over here. The vortex seems to be centered in this area…

TY. *(By bookcase)* But most of the stuff has been happening over here.

MADAME ROSA. *(Quickly crossing to bookcase)* Oh yes, yes, I feel it getting stronger, stronger…! Oh, my! It's strongest right here. It was leaking over a bit into that area but this, this is most definitely the source.

MRS. WILLIAMS. What does it want?

MADAME ROSA. We must have…a seance!

> (**MADAME ROSA** *closes the curtains, dims the lights.*)

MADAME ROSA. Everyone gather around here in a circle and join hands.

> *(They do.)*

MADAME ROSA. Now, we must all concentrate very hard and whatever happens, do not speak and do not break the chain.

MAGGIE. Mommy, I'm scared.

MRS. WILLIAMS. I'm right here, darling, I won't let anything happen to you.

MADAME ROSA. Now we begin. *(Closes her eyes)* Spirit of this house, we wish to contact you. Let us ease your pain and release you from this place. *(She sighs dramatically.)*

BECKA. *(Unimpressed)* That's just what *we* were doing.

MADAME ROSA. Quiet! Now, where was I? Lonely soul who is trapped here, come forward, come forward. We wish only peace for you.

(The lights flicker. Gasps of amazement.)

BECKA. I don't like this.

SUZE. I think I hear my mother calling…

MADAME ROSA. Do not break the circle! Shadow of what once was, we are here for you. Tell us what we can do to help you. What do you want?

(A faint sorrowful cry.)

MR. WILLIAMS. Wow, she's good.

MADAME ROSA. We are listening, we only want to help…

(A few notes of someone humming "Follow The Drinking Gourd.")

MR. WILLIAMS. She's *really* good.

MADAME ROSA. Speak! Speak now! What do you want?!

(A loud cry and several books jump out of the bookcase. The lights go out. A loud cry of fright from **MADAME ROSA.** *)*

MADAME ROSA. Let me out of here!

(The lights snap back on. **MADAME ROSA** *is running toward the front door.)*

MRS. WILLIAMS. Madame Rosa! What's the matter?

MADAME ROSA. Are you crazy? This place is haunted!

*(**MADAME ROSA** exits.)*

Blackout

Scene Four

(1855.)

(The books have been replaced and the room returned to normal. It is early evening. **MR. JAMESON** *and* **ELIJAH** *are working on the bookcase door and the little room behind it.)*

MR. JAMESON. What say you, Master Carpenter?

ELIJAH. It's wonderful, Papa! There's plenty of room and the kitchen looks perfectly normal.

MR. JAMESON. It had better look perfectly normal. One small mistake could cost someone their life.

*(***TEMPERANCE*** runs in through the front door, holding her doll.)*

TEMPERANCE. Papa! Reverend Matthews is coming! He's riding up on Old Chestnut. May Miss Alice feed him a carrot?

MR. JAMESON. Who, Reverend Matthews?

TEMPERANCE. No, silly, Old Chestnut.

MR. JAMESON. Go and see if there's one left in the vegetable bin. Where is your mother?

TEMPERANCE. *(Exiting to kitchen)* Taking down the laundry.

ELIJAH. Let's play a trick on him, Papa. Let's hide in here and see if he can find us.

REVEREND MATTHEWS. *(O.S.)* Hello? Thomas? Elijah? Are you there?

MR. JAMESON. Hurry!

*(***MR. JAMESON*** and ***ELIJAH*** enter the closet. ***TEMPER-ANCE*** enters with a carrot.)*

TEMPERANCE. May I give him this one?

MR. JAMESON. That's fine.

*(***TEMPERANCE*** exits out front door. ***MR. JAMESON*** closes the bookcase.)*

REVEREND MATTHEWS. *(O.S.)* Hello, Temperance. Where's your father?

TEMPERANCE. *(O.S.)* He's in there. Here, Old Chestnut!

> (**REVEREND MATTHEWS** *enters through front door carrying a Bible.*)

REVEREND MATTHEWS. Thomas? Hello? Are you here?

> (**REVEREND MATTHEWS** *looks around, exits to kitchen.* **MR. JAMESON** *enters from bookcase, closes it behind him.*)

REVEREND MATTHEWS. *(O.S.)* Thomas?

> (**REVEREND MATTHEWS** *re-enters.*)

REVEREND MATTHEWS. *(Surprised to see* **MR. JAMESON***)* Oh, there you are! I didn't hear you come in.

MR. JAMESON. I didn't come in. I was here all along.

REVEREND MATTHEWS. This is no time for games, Thomas. I have come on urgent business.

MR. JAMESON. It's not a game, Reverend. It's a test. We have just finished building a hiding place in this very room and wished to try it out. Look closely. Can you spot it?

REVEREND MATTHEWS. *(Looking around)* No, you seem to have made a fine job of it.

MR. JAMESON. Here, let me show…

REVEREND MATTHEWS. No, it is better that I not know. What I do not know, I cannot tell.

MR. JAMESON. Very wise. Look away, then.

> (**REVEREND MATTHEWS** *closes his eyes.* **MR. JAMESON** *opens the bookcase,* **ELIJAH** *enters and the bookcase is closed again.*)

ELIJAH. Good evening, Reverend. It's almost like magic, isn't it?

REVEREND MATTHEWS. *(Uncovering eyes)* It's a miracle on order with the loaves and fishes.

ELIJAH. It's only a door.

REVEREND MATTHEWS. Only a door that your father has built to hide slaves. His decision to join us is the real wonder, by the grace of God.

MR. JAMESON. God and my wife.

REVEREND MATTHEWS. Speaking of which, Elijah, would you be so good as to fetch your mother and sisters? What I have to say must be heard by all of you.

ELIJAH. Yes, sir.

(**ELIJAH** *exits out front door.*)

REVEREND MATTHEWS. I'm afraid we must trouble you for your services much sooner than we would like.

MR. JAMESON. Runaway slaves are coming now?!

REVEREND MATTHEWS. Normally, we would not ask it of you until you had had some instruction but this is an emergency.

MR. JAMESON. And the children?

REVEREND MATTHEWS. It is best that they be told as much as possible so they are prepared. Since they are going to be involved, they must be made aware of the importance of secrecy and what to do in the event something should, heaven forbid, go wrong.

MR. JAMESON. God save us all if something goes wrong.

(*Enter through the front door* **MRS. JAMESON**, **TEMPER- ANCE**, **FAITH** *and* **ELIJAH**. *As usual,* **TEMPERANCE** *carries her doll.*)

MRS. JAMESON. Good evening, Reverend Matthews. May I offer you some refreshment?

REVEREND MATTHEWS. Thank you but there isn't time, Mrs. Jameson. You are expecting visitors.

MRS. JAMESON. Visitors? Oh! You mean runaways? But we're not ready!

REVEREND MATTHEWS. No one is ever truly ready the first time. But from now on, you must always be prepared. That is rule number one – be prepared. Children, do you understand what is going to happen?

TEMPERANCE. Slaves are coming to hide with us.

REVEREND MATTHEWS. Yes and it is of the utmost importance that you not tell anyone. (*He holds out his Bible.*) Will you swear to God on His holy book that you will keep it a secret?

TEMPERANCE, FAITH, ELIJAH. *(Putting their hands on the Bible)* We swear.

REVEREND MATTHEWS. Very good. Because rule number one is secrecy.

ELIJAH. I thought rule number one was be prepared.

REVEREND MATTHEWS. I forgot. Very well, rule number one is be prepared and rule number two is secrecy.

FAITH. What's rule number three?

REVEREND MATTHEWS. Not to ask questions!

MRS. JAMESON. How many are coming, Reverend?

FAITH. Are there any children?

ELIJAH. How long will they stay?

TEMPERANCE. Where did they come from?

MR. JAMESON. What happened to rule number three?

REVEREND MATTHEWS. Word has just reached me that passengers are coming tonight so I hung a lit lantern on your gate to let them know they may enter. If you are ever expecting passengers and it is not safe, you must not light the lantern. That is the sign of danger on the Underground Railroad.

TEMPERANCE. If we're part of a railroad, will a locomotive come through our house?

REVEREND MATTHEWS. No, Temperance, it's not a real railroad but a way for slaves to travel to freedom. Like the railroad, we call the slaves who travel on it passengers. Agents help them escape from their masters down south and start them on their journey. Conductors travel with them to safe houses we call stations. You are station masters because your house is a station. I will tell you the location of the next station but that is all. Then, if you are ever caught, you can't give away the whole network.

MRS. JAMESON. That's very clever.

REVEREND MATTHEWS. Yes but it all depends on you. You must always be on your guard. Just one wrong word and you and the passengers will be in terrible danger. They'll be arriving soon. What provisions have you made for them?

MR. JAMESON. The hidden room is finished, praise God.

MRS. JAMESON. And we've made up a cozy space in the barn hidden by a wall of hay bales.

TEMPERANCE. And if anyone finds it, we are to say it's our fort.

ELIJAH. And there's the cold cellar down under the barn.

FAITH. And we found a cave in the woods they can stay in, too.

TEMPERANCE. And they can wear my pink Sunday dress if they need to. I won't mind. *(Whispering to* **REVEREND MATTHEWS***)* I don't like it.

REVEREND MATTHEWS. That all sounds most excellent. What is the number one rule?

ALL BUT REVEREND MATTHEWS. Be prepared!

REVEREND MATTHEWS. Secrecy!

(The sound of someone singing "Follow The Drinking Gourd" outside the front door.)

REVEREND MATTHEWS. *(With a nervous start)* Shhh!

(A knock at the front door.)

MRS. JAMESON. Is that them?

REVEREND MATTHEWS. It is. That song is another sign.

MRS. JAMESON. I'm so nervous!

REVEREND MATTHEWS. *(Nervously)* Try to remain calm.

MR. JAMESON. It's hard when we're about to break the law.

MRS. JAMESON. *(Bravely)* We break man's law to uphold God's law.

REVEREND MATTHEWS. Amen!

TEMPERANCE. Shouldn't someone answer the door?

*(***REVEREND MATTHEWS*** opens his Bible.)*

MRS. JAMESON. Yes. A prayer to bless our new endeavor.

*(***REVEREND MATTHEWS*** takes a pistol out of the hollow book.)*

REVEREND MATTHEWS. Some situations call for something a

little stronger than prayer.

(**REVEREND MATTHEWS** *opens the front door with the gun hidden behind his back.*)

MR. COLLINS. *(O.S.)* Good evening.

REVEREND MATTHEWS. Good evening to you, sir.

MR. COLLINS. *(O.S.)* I am a friend of a friend.

REVEREND MATTHEWS. *(Returning gun to book)* Then you are most welcome here.

(**MR. COLLINS, FAST, SLOW,** *and* **CALICO** *enter.* **MR. COLLINS** *supports* **CALICO** *for SHE is ill.*)

MRS. JAMESON. Oh, she's ill, poor thing. Put her on the settee.

(**CALICO** *is deposited on the couch.*)

MRS. JAMESON. *(Crossing to couch and checking* **CALICO***)* Lie back, dear. She has a fever. Temperance, run and soak a cold cloth. Elijah, fetch a nice hot brick from the stove and wrap it in a flannel. Faith, please bring that lemonade, there's a good girl.

(**FAITH, TEMPERANCE** *and* **ELIJAH** *exit to kitchen.* **MRS. JAMESON** *puts a quilt on* **CALICO***.*)

MR. COLLINS. She's been poorly since our first night out. Her brothers here have taken care of her but I'm afraid she's gotten worse.

MRS. JAMESON. Thank Jesus Lord you got here when you did. What's your name, dear?

CALICO. *(Quietly)* Calico, ma'am.

MRS. JAMESON. You don't feel so well, do you, Calico.

CALICO. No ma'am.

MRS. JAMESON. We'll fix that in a jiffy. *(To* **FAST** *and* **SLOW***)* What do they call you boys?

FAST. I'm Fast, ma'am and he's Slow.

MRS. JAMESON. Those aren't proper Christian names. Why do they call you that?

FAST. Master says that's what we are. *(Indicates himself)* Fast. *(Indicates* **SLOW***)* Slow.

(TEMPERANCE enters with a cloth. MRS. JAMESON puts it on CALICO's forehead.)

MRS. JAMESON. There. I'll warrant that feels good.

REVEREND MATTHEWS. *(To MR. COLLINS)* This is Mr. and Mrs. Jameson. You're their first passengers.

MR. COLLINS. *(Shaking hands with MR. JAMESON)* Jebediah Collins. Mighty pleased to meet you. *(Tips hat to MRS. JAMESON)* Ma'am. Praise the Lord you've signed on. We could use a hundred more with your courage.

MR. JAMESON. You're most welcome in our home.

REVEREND MATTHEWS. How many are you?

MR. COLLINS. Three men, two women and the youngins. This being our first time here, I thought it best to keep the others hidden until I was sure things was safe.

(Enter FAITH with a tray carrying cups and a pitcher. She pours lemonade for COLLINS, FAST, SLOW and CALICO.)

MR. COLLINS, FAST, SLOW. Much obliged, ma'am, thank you kindly, etc.

MR. JAMESON. Let me show you where you'll be staying. There'll be supper soon as it's ready.

MR. COLLINS. Hot food will be mighty welcome. We've been living pretty rough out in the woods.

MRS. JAMESON. Thomas, take the lemonade out to the others. They'll want a cold drink, too.

(MR. JAMESON takes the pitcher and cups and exits out front door with MR. COLLINS and REVEREND MATTHEWS.)

MRS. JAMESON. There, now. It's nice and quiet. How's that lemonade? Good?

(Enter ELIJAH with a brick wrapped in cloth. MRS. JAMESON puts it at CALICO's feet.)

MRS. JAMESON. We'll put this hot brick down here to warm up those cold feet.

CALICO. Thank you kindly, ma'am. I feel like I'm floating on a cloud up in heaven.

MRS. JAMESON. You just float there as long as you please. *(She takes a bit of ribbon from her pocket and puts it in **CAL-ICO**'s hair.)* There. Can't go floating around up in by heaven unless you're as pretty as an angel. I'm going to see to supper. The children will keep you company. You just tell them if you need anything.

*(**MRS. JAMESON** exits to kitchen.)*

ELIJAH. *(To **FAST** and **SLOW**)* Have you really been sleeping outside in the woods every night?

FAST. The woods, the fields, the swamps, wherever we can.

SLOW. One night, we burrowed down right inside a haystack and I put my hand directly on a grass snake. You probably heard my scream way up here I was so surprised.

ELIJAH. Aren't you scared of haunts?

SLOW. Powerful scared. But I got me a lucky charm against them.

*(**SLOW** shows his charm.)*

SLOW. Old Sister carved it up for me herself from a horse chestnut and put a spell on it. So now nothing can harm me.

(The others are impressed.)

TEMPERANCE. Then why were you so scared of the snake?

SLOW. I knew it works on haunts. Didn't know if it worked on snakes. He didn't bite me so I guess it does.

FAITH. You're awful brave.

FAST. Haunts and snakes ain't nothing up against what we running from and what we running to. Ain't nothing gonna make us go back and nothing keeping us from going forward.

ELIJAH. Why – what's behind you?

FAST. Master with a whip.

TEMPERANCE. And what's ahead?

FAST. Ma waiting for us in freedom up in Canada.

FAITH. How come your mama's not with you?

FAST. Master sold her and then she run away. She were working to buy our freedom but she say it take too long.

SLOW. So she send word we should run away to her ourselves.

ELIJAH. What about your Papa?

FAST. He waiting for us somewhere else. We be seeing him later.

ELIJAH. When?

SLOW. Don't rightly know. But not for a long time, I hope.

TEMPERANCE. Why's that? Where is he?

CALICO. Heaven.

TEMPERANCE. That's sad.

CALICO. But he's watching down on us right now and keeping us safe and helping us get back with Ma again.

TEMPERANCE. You believe in heaven, too?

ELIJAH. Temperance! 'Course they believe in heaven! They're not heathen savages from the wilderness.

TEMPERANCE. Well, I don't know. I never met a real honest-to-goodness slave before.

ELIJAH. Haven't you been listening to Reverend Matthews on Sunday? He says all the time how they're just like us except their skin's darker.

FAITH. Except here. I saw when you took your lemonade.

*(***FAITH*** *holds up her palm.* ***FAST*** *holds up his palm and they compare.)*

FAST. Just the same color.

*(***FAST*** *puts his palm against* ***FAITH****'s.* ***SLOW*** *holds up his palm and joins it to* ***ELIJAH****'s.* ***TEMPERANCE*** *and* ***CALICO*** *put their palms together.*

FAITH. Do you like kittens? We got some in the barn.

ELIJAH. And Papa and I built a tree house out back – you can come and see it. And we built this cupboard hidden behind here to hide you in if someone comes looking.

*(***ELIJAH*** *opens the bookcase door.)*

FAST. You're a good carpenter.

ELIJAH. Wait 'til you see the tree house!

FAITH. And the kittens!

(**FAITH**, **ELIJAH**, **FAST** *and* **SLOW** *exit out front door.*)

CALICO. I wish I could go out.

TEMPERANCE. That's the good thing about kittens – you don't have to go to them, they can come in and see you if they have a mind to. And you can climb up into the tree house when you're feeling better. *(She tries to think of something to say.)* Miss Alice is scared of climbing up there sometimes. She's afraid she'll fall.

CALICO. Who's Miss Alice?

TEMPERANCE. *(Holding her out)* She is. Say hello, Miss Alice. She's mighty pleased to meet you.

CALICO. Hello to you, Miss Alice. She's awful pretty. She's probably about the prettiest doll baby I ever saw.

TEMPERANCE. Would you like to hold her for a while? She wouldn't mind.

(**TEMPERANCE** *hands the doll to* **CALICO**.)

CALICO. I ain't never had a doll baby like this before.

TEMPERANCE. Papa made her for me. Maybe he could make one for you, too.

CALICO. *(Handing doll back)* It sure would help keep me from being scared hiding out there in the night. Those boys talk so brave but they every bit as scared as me. I don't like the dark.

TEMPERANCE. Neither do I.

CALICO. I sure hope I don't have to go in that closet there – it looks powerful dark. And powerful small. I don't like being shut up in small places like that.

(**TEMPERANCE** *and* **CALICO** *look at the bookcase.*)

TEMPERANCE. But if you had to hide, it's the safest place.

(**TEMPERANCE** *opens the bookcase wider.*)

TEMPERANCE. Maybe you should just get into it a little bit, just to get used to it.

CALICO. I couldn't do that! I'd be so scared, I'd like to die! It's like some old graveyard bone house!

TEMPERANCE. Don't be afraid. Miss Alice and I will be right here.

(**CALICO** *stands just inside the bookcase doorway.*)

CALICO. How's this?

TEMPERANCE. Look how brave you are!

CALICO. I am! I am brave! Look!

(**CALICO** *takes a step more into the space.*)

TEMPERANCE. And you aren't scared? Not even a little bit?

CALICO. Not even a little. Well, maybe a tiny bit.

TEMPERANCE. What if I… ?

(**TEMPERANCE** *begins to close the door.*)

CALICO. Oh, please don't do that! I couldn't bear it, honestly I couldn't!

TEMPERANCE. But you might have to, if someone comes. You wouldn't want to be caught and have to go back to being a slave again, would you?

CALICO. No, ma'am, I wouldn't but I don't think I'd be thinking about that if you shut that door. I'd just go plumb out of my head crazy being in here all alone.

TEMPERANCE. What if you had Miss Alice with you to keep you company?

(**TEMPERANCE** *hands the doll to* **CALICO**.)

TEMPERANCE. How's that?

CALICO. She sure does make me feel right better. I think maybe…

(**ELIJAH** *enters through the front door at a run.*)

ELIJAH. Papa! Mama! Someone's coming up the path!

TEMPERANCE. Now you have to stay in there! Hold on to Miss Alice tight and don't make a sound!

(**TEMPERANCE** *shuts the bookcase door.*)

Blackout

End of Act One

ACT TWO

SCENE ONE

(Today, three days later. The room is in shadow, the only light comes in through the window. There is a briefcase by the couch. A figure wrapped in a piece of fabric is flailing about the room, muttering loudly. The front door opens. Enter the **WILLIAMS** *family.* **TY, MAGGIE** *and* **JANIE** *see the "ghost" and immediately begin shouting.)*

MAGGIE. Mommy!

JANIE. It's the ghost!

TY. Get him!

*(*TY, **MAGGIE** *and* JANIE *rush at the ghost and tackle him to the floor.)*

MRS. WILLIAMS. *(Turning on the lights)* Children! For heaven's sake! It's not a ghost!

GHOST. *(Tangled in his sheet)* Help! Help!

MR. WILLIAMS. That's not a ghost – it's a Porterfoy! Kids, it's okay, let her go. She's the one we came to meet.

*(***MR. WILLIAMS** *pulls the kids off the ghost and removes the curtains. Underneath is a very rumpled* **PROFESSOR PORTERFOY.***)*

PROFESSOR PORTERFOY. My goodness! And people think being a historian is safe and dull. A ghost...hmmph!

MRS. WILLIAMS. I'm so sorry. This place has got us a bit on edge. We had to stay at a hotel the last two nights.

JANIE. If you're not a ghost, why were you trying to scare us?

PROFESSOR PORTERFOY. I wasn't trying to scare you.

TY. Then why were you wearing a sheet?

PROFESSOR PORTERFOY. I was trying to open the drapes so I could see properly and I'm afraid I got a bit tangled up. *(Holding out her hand)* Professor Margaret Porterfoy, head of the local historic society. Your husband told me you were interested in the history of your house. I thought I'd come in and take a look around before you got here. If I'd known it would result in an attack by wild savages, I would've stayed at home.

JANIE. It's not wild savages you have to be afraid of. It's the ghost.

PROFESSOR PORTERFOY. So there's a ghost, is there?

MAGGIE. Of the dead poisoned dog we found in the oven.

TY. Do you believe in ghosts?

PROFESSOR PORTERFOY. I believe that you believe there's a ghost.

JANIE. But we've seen it!

TY. Well, heard it.

MAGGIE. And the Cyclops said it was here, too.

PROFESSOR PORTERFOY. Cyclops?

MRS. WILLIAMS. Psychic. I'm afraid she only made things worse.

TY. And stuff happens. Books jump off the shelves…

MAGGIE. It took my Barbie!

JANIE. And something knocks in the walls…

MAGGIE. And we all sing a song!

PROFESSOR PORTERFOY. You all sing a song?

MR. WILLIAMS. It's the oddest thing – we'd never heard it before we moved in and now we can't seem to get it out of our heads.

(*The family hums a bit of "Follow The Drinking Gourd."*)

PROFESSOR PORTERFOY. Why, that's extraordinary!

MR. WILLIAMS. Well, we're not professional entertainers or anything…

PROFESSOR PORTERFOY. No, no! It's amazing that you know it! That's "Follow The Drinking Gourd."

JANIE. What's a drinking gourd?

TY. And why are we supposed to follow it?

PROFESSOR PORTERFOY. It's an old song from before the Civil War. It was a way to give directions to slaves escaping north. It just sounded like any old folk song but it was really a secret code. It hasn't been well-known for over a hundred years!

JANIE. That proves there's a ghost – if he didn't tell it to us, how could we sing it?

TY. What's the secret code?

(**PROFESSOR PORTERFOY** *crosses to get her brief case, sits on the couch and opens it, referring to papers inside as she talks.*)

PROFESSOR PORTERFOY. "The Drinking Gourd" refers to the Big Dipper. The escaping slaves were to walk in the direction of the Big Dipper, which was north in the winter sky.

TY. What other secret stuff did they do?

PROFESSOR PORTERFOY. Well, they had code words to recognize one other. For instance, if someone said that he was a friend of a friend. Since the Quakers, the religious Society of Friends, helped start the Railroad in 1780, a friend of a Friend meant someone who was on the side of abolition.

MR. WILLIAMS. Abolition was the belief that slavery was wrong and should be abolished or wiped out.

PROFESSOR PORTERFOY. *(Dropping papers all over)* Oopsydaisy! *(Gathering the papers)* And there's a very interesting theory that women sewed quilts with designs on them showing escape routes. They could hang them out on wash lines and those who knew the secret would know where to travel next. But this idea hasn't been proven to my satisfaction yet.

MRS. WILLIAMS. How do you know all this?

PROFESSOR PORTERFOY. It's my specialty, Mrs. Williams. I've done quite a bit of research at the local level as this whole area was rife with Railroad activity. That's why your husband thought I could help.

(She picks up a paper she is stepping on and rips it.)

PROFESSOR PORTERFOY. Oh dear!

MRS. WILLIAMS. And can you?

PROFESSOR PORTERFOY. Can I what? Oh! Help you. Yes! Did you know this house was a station on the Underground Railroad?

TY. Cool! We studied that in school! Did Harriet Tubman stay here?

PROFESSOR PORTERFOY. I don't believe so but other slaves most certainly did.

MAGGIE. Who's Harry The Tub Man?

PROFESSOR PORTERFOY. Harriet Tubman was a slave who escaped from her master in Maryland and returned to the South 15 times to help others escape.

MR. WILLIAMS. Were you able to find out anything about the people who lived here?

PROFESSOR PORTERFOY. Oh, yes, there were quite a few documents. Let's see…*(She drops more papers)*…the place was originally built in 1845 by a farmer named Thomas Jameson. He was married with three children…

JANIE. Just like us!

PROFESSOR PORTERFOY. In 1855, they joined the Underground Railroad and this house became a safe haven on the road to freedom.

TY. So he was a hero like George Washington.

PROFESSOR PORTERFOY. It was very dangerous to help escaping slaves, you understand. If you were caught, you were fined and put in prison. One fellow, Thomas Garrett, a businessman in Delaware, was caught helping slaves and fined over $5,000 but that didn't stop him from continuing to work on the Railroad for 40 years.

MRS. WILLIAMS. Amazing! To think this house is a part of history.

MR. WILLIAMS. Makes you appreciate it a little more, doesn't it, wet raccoon smell and all?

PROFESSOR PORTERFOY. My favorite conductor was John Fairfield from Cincinnati. He hired a hearse and disguised 28 slaves as the funeral procession and got them away without anyone being the wiser.

TY. That was pretty smart.

PROFESSOR PORTERFOY. Not all escaping slaves rode the Railroad, of course. One fellow, Henry Brown, had himself shipped from Virginia to Philadelphia in a wooden box.

JANIE. He mailed himself?

PROFESSOR PORTERFOY. Exactly.

MRS. WILLIAMS. That's all very interesting but what does it have to do with our ghost?

PROFESSOR PORTERFOY. *(Taking an old book from her briefcase)* Maybe everything. This diary was written by Mrs. Jameson herself.

*(She almost drops it but **MRS. WILLIAMS** catches it.)*

PROFESSOR PORTERFOY. Oopsy-daisy!

MRS. WILLIAMS. *(Wonderingly)* Imagine! The thoughts of a woman who lived here all those years ago…it could be me…

MR. WILLIAMS. Forget it. I am not buying you 150 years of past birthday presents.

JANIE. How can some boring old diary help us get rid of our ghost?

PROFESSOR PORTERFOY. I think it might be just what you need. Read where I've marked, if you please.

MRS. WILLIAMS. *(Opening diary at bookmark and reading)* August 10, 1855. It's been three days since the children arrived on our doorstep. The others left the following morning but due to Calico's ill health, she has stayed behind with Fast and Slow.

*(A light change. **MRS. JAMESON** enters. The modern characters fade back.)*

MRS. JAMESON & MRS. WILLIAMS. We all recognize how extremely dangerous this is…

MRS. JAMESON. *(Taking the diary, writing in it and reading alone)*…yet we cannot bear to force the girl on her way while she is poorly and the boys will not leave her. But she is stronger every day and it is with a heavy heart that we must very soon say goodbye to them.

(The modern characters exit to the kitchen. Enter **CALICO** *and* **TEMPERANCE** *through the front door.* **MRS. JAMESON** *puts the diary away and hums "Follow The Drinking Gourd.")*

CALICO. …and my doll baby will fly through the air to freedom! She won't have to take no secret trail.

TEMPERANCE. Mama, have you seen Miss Alice?

MRS. JAMESON. No, dear, I'm afraid I haven't.

TEMPERANCE. We can't find her anywhere and Papa is still working on a doll for Calico. Isn't it wonderful of him?

MRS. JAMESON. I hope you both thanked him properly.

TEMPERANCE. Oh, we did, a million times.

CALICO. Yes, ma'am, truly. I never had nothing beautiful for my own self. I already gave her a name. She's gonna be Miss Marmalade.

MRS. JAMESON. You seem to be feeling much better today.

*(***CALICO** *exchanges a glance with* **TEMPERANCE** *and coughs unconvincingly.)*

CALICO. I dare say I feel a little fainting spell coming on me now, I think.

TEMPERANCE. She's still trying to get over the shock of being in the secret room all alone and thinking someone was coming to get her.

MRS. JAMESON. We were lucky it was just Reverend Matthews' wife coming to see how we were getting along.

TEMPERANCE. *(Elbowing* **CALICO***)* Miss Alice kept her from dying of fright but she still had a pretty nasty shock.

CALICO. Yes, ma'am, I'm still shocked.

MRS. JAMESON. Well, that's a shame because I was going to ask you two to help me bake some cookies but if you have to go lie down…

TEMPERANCE. Oh, I think baking cookies might help her feel stronger, Mama.

CALICO. *Eating* cookies sure would.

MRS. JAMESON. Then you girls go wash your hands and I'll be right in.

TEMPERANCE. Yes, Mama.

CALICO. Yes, ma'am.

(**TEMPERANCE** *and* **CALICO** *exit to kitchen.* **MRS. JAMESON** *crosses to the front door, opens it, calls out.*)

MRS. JAMESON. Faith! We want to start the cookies! Bring in that butter soon as you've finished churning!

ELIJAH, FAST, SLOW. *(Off)* Cookies?!

(**MRS. JAMESON** *stands to one side.* **ELIJAH, FAST** *and* **SLOW** *run in. We can't see it but* **ELIJAH** *has Miss Alice hidden behind his back, stuck in the waistband of his pants and covered with his shirt.*)

ELIJAH. Who's got cookies?

MRS. JAMESON. Nobody yet but you'll be the first to know when we do. Have you boys finished your chores?

ELIJAH, FAST, SLOW. Yes, ma'am.

MRS. JAMESON. Run along and play then, and I'll call you when the cookies are ready.

(**MRS. JAMESON** *starts to exit to kitchen, turns back.*)

MRS. JAMESON. You boys haven't seen Miss Alice anywhere, have you?

(*The* **BOYS** *look at one another.*)

ELIJAH. Didn't Temperance have her at breakfast?

MRS. JAMESON. I don't know but she's missing now so keep any eye out for her, all right?

ELIJAH, FAST, SLOW. Yes, ma'am.

(**MRS. JAMESON** *exits to kitchen.*)

ELIJAH. *(Taking Miss Alice out)* Boy, that was close!

FAST. Why you go and lie to your Ma like that?

ELIJAH. I didn't lie. I never said I didn't *have* her.

FAST. You know what she mean.

SLOW. And how come we carrying around that old doll for anyway? What for you want to be playing with some girl's doll?

ELIJAH. To make Temperance mad.

SLOW. How's that fun?

FAST. No game making your sister cry and carry on. And when your Ma and Pa find out we had something to do with it, we gonna get a whipping for sure.

ELIJAH. *(Quickly trying to think of something else)* I mean, we're going to play a game with it.

FAST. What game?

ELIJAH. *(Looking around)* Pirates! You two are pirates that come on board my ship, which is here on the settee and I'm the captain and I've got to try to fend you off and save the beautiful maiden who is locked in my cabin which is the hiding cupboard.

(**ELIJAH** *opens the secret door of the bookcase and puts Miss Alice inside on the floor.*)

SLOW. Pirates! That's a fine game!

ELIJAH. So go on now, try to capture me!

(*The BOYS plays at pirates. Enter* **CALICO** *and* **TEMPERANCE** *from the kitchen.*)

TEMPERANCE. I don't know how it can take one person so long to churn a little butter.

CALICO. I can do it myself quick as a lick. I done it lots of times.

(**ELIJAH** *crosses to stand in front of the secret cupboard.*)

TEMPERANCE. What are you doing?

ELIJAH. Just playing.

TEMPERANCE. Where's Miss Alice, Elijah? I know you stole her.

ELIJAH. I don't have your stupid, old doll.

TEMPERANCE. I'm going to tell Mama you're playing in the house if you don't give her back to me and you'll get a licking. You know Papa doesn't want you…

(Enter **MR. JAMESON** *through the front door.)*

MR. JAMESON. Papa doesn't want you what?

ELIJAH. Playing in the secret cupboard.

MR. JAMESON. Then why do you persist in doing so?

ELIJAH. We're sorry.

MR. JAMESON. *(Shutting the secret door)* I know it's very tempting but it mustn't get damaged. I don't want anyone playing about in it.

FAST & SLOW. Sorry, sir.

MR. JAMESON. Now go on and play outside.

*(***ELIJAH** *and* **TEMPERANCE** *trade faces with each other behind* **MR. JAMESON***'s back.* **ELIJAH**, **FAST** *and* **SLOW** *exit out front door.)*

MR. JAMESON. And what are you girls supposed to be doing?

TEMPERANCE. Getting butter from Faith to make cookies.

MR. JAMESON. You'd better do it, then. How are you feeling today, Miss Calico?

CALICO. Much…*(a look from* **TEMPERANCE***)*…a *little* better, thank you, sir.

MR. JAMESON. That's good to hear. You look very pretty with that ribbon in your hair. Go on, now, scat!

*(***TEMPERANCE** *and* **CALICO** *exit out the front door.)*

TEMPERANCE. *(Exiting)* Elijah Jameson, you give me back my doll!

*(***MRS. JAMESON** *enters from kitchen.)*

MRS. JAMESON. Temperance, we can't do anything until…

Oh, I thought you were Temperance.

MR. JAMESON. I sent her on her way. She seems to think Elijah took Miss Alice.

MRS. JAMESON. He might have. He's been acting up these last few days. I think having other boys around has gotten him in rather high spirits.

MR. JAMESON. It's been nice having them here, hasn't it? I know we're taking a terrible risk by not sending them on but it's such a joy watching them come out of their shells and finding happiness in the smallest things.

MRS. JAMESON. It breaks my heart to see the look they get sometimes when they draw back from us for no reason, expecting to be barked at and ordered about.

MR. JAMESON. I suppose we really must make them leave, for their safety as well as our own. You know how Temperance is. She wouldn't tell anything on purpose but she is such a little chatterbox. Yesterday in town, I saw her babbling away to Mrs. Patterson and the Lord only knows what she might have let slip. I'm going to speak to Reverend Matthews this afternoon.

MRS. JAMESON. *(With a sigh)* I shall hate to see them go.

MR. JAMESON. Now don't turn into a broody hen on me, Mother. I'm too old to stay up all night with a new baby.

MRS. JAMESON. Since when did you ever stay up all night with any baby, Thomas Jameson? And besides, if the Lord wishes us to have another child, we must follow His design without complaint.

MR. JAMESON. You've been known to make a suggestion to the Lord now and again, I seem to remember. Now are we going to enjoy fresh cookies today or aren't we?

(**MRS. JAMESON** *gives* **MR. JAMESON** *a kiss. Enter* **FAITH**, *carrying butter,* **CALICO** *and* **TEMPERANCE**.)

TEMPERANCE. *(Seeing her parents)* Kissing! *(SHE makes a disgusted sound)*

FAITH. I've finished the butter. If *you're* quite finished, we can start the cookies.

(**FAITH** *holds out the butter.*)

MR. JAMESON. You heard her.

(**MR. JAMESON** *exits out front door.* **MRS. JAMESON** *takes the butter and exits to kitchen. Tired,* **FAITH** *sits on the couch.*)

TEMPERANCE. Faith, have you seen Miss Alice?

FAITH. No. Go ask Elijah. He's probably got her.

TEMPERANCE. He says he doesn't.

CALICO. He was acting awful funny when we came in before. He ran and stood right in front of the secret door like he was hiding something.

TEMPERANCE. Maybe he put her in there.

(**TEMPERANCE** *opens the bookcase door.* **CALICO** *grabs up the doll and hugs it.*)

TEMPERANCE. Miss Alice! There you are, poor thing! That naughty Elijah, wait until I tell Mama…

MRS. JAMESON. *(O.S.)* Are you girls going to come help me or…

(**MR. JAMESON** *enters through front door very agitated.*)

MR. JAMESON. Elizabeth! There are two men coming up the walk!

MRS. JAMESON. *(Entering from kitchen)* Who are they?

MR. JAMESON. It may be those two bounty hunters again. Faith, run out back and find the boys and tell them to hide in the hay loft. Calico, into the secret cupboard with you. Don't make a sound!

(**FAITH** *exits through the kitchen.* **CALICO** *goes into the secret room still clutching the doll.* **MR. JAMESON** *shuts the bookcase door.*)

MR. JAMESON. Temperance, run and stay on the back porch, please.

TEMPERANCE. But Miss Alice…

MR. JAMESON. …will be fine in there! Now do as I say!

(**TEMPERANCE** *exits to kitchen.*)

MR. JAMESON. We must act completely normal. They have no reason to suspect anything. A knock at the front door.

(**MR. JAMESON** *and* **MRS. JAMESON** *look around to make sure that nothing is out of place.* **MR. JAMESON** *crosses to the front door and opens it.*)

SLATTERY. *(Bursting in, carrying a rifle)* Remember us?

COOMBS. *(Bursting in with a rifle)* Your old friends?

MR. JAMESON. I told you the last time, you have no business here.

SLATTERY. This time's different.

COOMBS. Different, yes. We got good reason to be here this time.

MR. JAMESON. You have no proof that we…

COOMBS. No proof, no…

SLATTERY. …but enough just cause to allow us to search you good and proper this time and you can't say boo about it.

MR. JAMESON. What cause?

SLATTERY. Your own daughter's words.

COOMBS. She was overheard talking about hiding runaways.

MRS. JAMESON. That's what you have? The imaginative ramblings of a child?

COOMBS. Imaginative ramblings, you say.

(**COOMBS** *exits to kitchen.*)

SLATTERY. Truth, we say.

MRS. JAMESON. Children make up things all the time. They live in a world of fantasy. Ours play at runaway slaves every day.

SLATTERY. This is no child's game. This is criminal lawlessness.

(*The crash of breaking glass from the kitchen.*)

MRS. JAMESON. *(Exiting to kitchen)* What is he doing?! Stop it at once!

MR. JAMESON. When the authorities hear what you are up to…

SLATTERY. Go on and fetch them, then. I shall be happy to speak to them.

(*More crashing from the kitchen.*)

MRS. JAMESON. (*O.S.*) Get out!

(**COOMBS** *enters from kitchen.*)

COOMBS. Kitchen's clear. No sign of them.

(**MRS. JAMESON** *enters from kitchen.*)

MRS. JAMESON. (*Planting herself in front of* **COOMBS**) Who is going to pay for that bowl of sugar?

COOMBS. Move aside.

MRS. JAMESON. Who is going to pay?!

(**COOMBS** *tries to push past* **MRS. JAMESON** *and bumps into her. She falls back with a cry.*)

MR. JAMESON. You dare lay hands on my wife, sir?!

(**MR. JAMESON** *pulls* **COOMBS** *away and spins him around.*)

SLATTERY. Leave off him, there!

(*There is pushing and shouting. Suddenly,* **ELIJAH**, **FAST** *and* **SLOW** *enter at a run through the kitchen doorway.*)

ELIJAH. Papa, we saw… !

SLATTERY. Oh ho! And what is this?!

MR. JAMESON. These are our farm hands, sir, hired on quite legally.

SLATTERY. Then you must have their papers showing that they have been properly set free.

MR. JAMESON. Yes, I do. If you will allow me to fetch them?

COOMBS. We don't have time for that.

SLATTERY. I think we'll just take them now and you can bring your documents into town when…

MR. JAMESON. You cannot simply take these boys because

you believe them to be escaped slaves. Wait here while I find their papers and you can leave us in peace once and for all.

(**MR. JAMESON** *exits to kitchen.* **SLATTERY** *gives* **COOMBS** *a look.* **COOMBS** *crosses and stands by the side of the kitchen doorway.*)

SLATTERY. *(To* **FAST***)* What's your name, boy?

FAST. Fast, sir.

SLATTERY. You a runaway slave, boy?

FAST. No, sir. I work for Mr. Jameson, sir.

SLATTERY. I don't think you're telling me the truth, boy. I think you're lying through your hat.

COOMBS. He's lying all right, Slats, plain as day.

SLATTERY. You know the punishment you get for lying to a white man? You get a whipping you won't soon forget.

ELIJAH. Don't you touch him!

SLATTERY. You shut your mouth, pup. I'll do what I please to runaway trash. *(To* **SLOW***)* What's your story, muddy?

SLOW. Ain't got no story, sir.

SLATTERY. Oh, I think you do. And I think it goes like this: Once upon a time, I had a nice master and then I got some uppity ideas about freedom and ran away. But then I got caught and sent back and after a whipping to teach me my lesson, I never set foot off my planta-tion again, the end. How's that sound, muddy?

COOMBS. That sounds about right to me, Slats.

SLOW. Don't know, sir.

SLATTERY. Don't know, sir, don't know, sir. *(He prods* **SLOW** *roughly.)* You sure are an ugly thing, ain't you?

ELIJAH. You leave him alone!

SLATTERY. One more word from you, pup, and I'll thrash him good!

MRS. JAMESON. Hush, Elijah! Don't make it worse.

SLATTERY. Don't make no difference what he does. It's gonna get a lot worse for you when they take you away to jail.

COOMBS. Take you all to jail!

SLOW. We ain't going back. We ain't slaves no more.

SLATTERY. Don't you sass me, muddy.

SLOW. And you better not hurt these nice folks.

SLATTERY. Or what you gonna do, boy? You gonna do something? You gonna come after me? (**SLATTERY** *pushes* **SLOW***'s shoulder.*)

COOMBS. You teach him, Slats! You teach him his manners good!

SLATTERY. You gonna make me sorry? (*HE pushes again*) This here little muddy gonna take me on?

(**SLATTERY** *pushes* **SLOW** *again.* **SLOW** *suddenly pushes away* **SLATTERY***'s hand.*)

SLATTERY. You musn't do that, boy!

(**SLATTERY** *slaps* **SLOW**. **SLOW** *cries out and falls down.* **CALICO** *bursts from the bookcase closet and throws herself at* **SLATTERY**, *dropping the doll.*)

CALICO. Leave him alone!

SLATTERY. My Lord, here's another one! They're coming out of the woodwork like lice!

(**SLATTERY** *is taken by surprise and in struggling to release himself from her, He swings himself around and strikes her in the head with the butt of his rifle.* **CALICO** *falls to the floor.* **MRS. JAMESON** *immediately crosses to her and kneels beside her.*

MRS. JAMESON. Calico!

COOMBS. I think she's taken a liking to you, Slats.

SLATTERY. Maybe I should buy this one for myself, Coombsie, what do you think?

MR. JAMESON. (*O.S.*) Gentlemen, this will prove they are free.

SLATTERY. (*To* **COOMBS**) Be ready, now. He might try something.

(**MR. JAMESON** *enters from kitchen carrying some papers.*)

MR. JAMESON. If you'll just look at these…

FAITH. *(Off from kitchen)* Papa! The slaves! They're running off from the barn!

TEMPERANCE. *(Off from kitchen)* Papa! Come quick! They're headed toward the woods!

SLATTERY. Go and see what's going on.

(**COOMBS** *exits to the kitchen.*)

MR. JAMESON. *(Crossing to* **SLATTERY***)* These are their releases from their masters.

(**MR. JAMESON** *drops the papers and grabs* **SLATTERY***'s gun. There is a struggle.*)

MR. JAMESON. Run, boys, run!

(**FAST** *and* **SLOW** *exit out the front door running fast.*)

SLATTERY. Damn you!

(**SLATTERY** *gains control of the gun and exits out the front door.*)

SLATTERY. *(Exiting)* Coombs! Coombs! Out here!

(There is a shot off.)

ELIJAH. Fast! Slow!

(**ELIJAH** *exits out front door.*)

MR. JAMESON. Elijah! Come back!

(**MR. JAMESON** *exits out front door.* **FAITH** *and* **TEMPERANCE** *enter from the kitchen.*)

FAITH. What's happening? Papa told us to shout…

TEMPERANCE. Mama, what is it? What's wrong with Calico?

MRS. JAMESON. She's taken an awful blow to the head. Girls, see if you can get her down to that cave you found…

(Another shot off.)

ELIJAH. *(O.S.)* Mama! Papa's been shot!

(**MRS. JAMESON** *exits through front door quickly. Shouts* *and noises off.)*

FAITH. Mama! Wait!

(**FAITH** *exits through front door at a run.)*

TEMPERANCE. Calico! You have to go to the cave! Remember the cave? You've got to go there right now!

CALICO. My poor head hurts something awful! It's pounding fit to burst!

TEMPERANCE. Hurry! We'll meet you later! At the cave!

(**TEMPERANCE** *scoops up her doll and exits out the front door. Left alone,* **CALICO** *sits up, holding her head.)*

CALICO. I feel awful bad. I don't think I can make it all that way. Maybe I'll just stay here and rest for a little bit.

(**CALICO** *crawls over to the bookcase door.)*

CALICO. Where's Miss Alice? Where's she got to? *(Puts her head in her hands)* If I could just stop this pounding…if I could just get to Ma and freedom…

(**CALICO** *crawls into the bookcase cupboard and closes the door behind her. The shouts and noises off gradually subside. Silence.)*

Fade Out

(Today.)

(The modern characters are just as they were when they began reading the diary. There is a general sigh – a release of tension. They all look around as if awakening from a dream.)

JANIE. And then what?

MRS. WILLIAMS. *(Looking at the book)* I don't know – the rest of it's blank.

TY. But what happened to them?

MAGGIE. Did they all get away and live happily ever after?

MR. WILLIAMS. You see how compelling history can be? What have I been telling you children all these years?

MRS. WILLIAMS. Why did she stop writing?

PROFESSOR PORTERFOY. I'm afraid she died.

MRS. WILLIAMS. Oh, no! That's terrible!

PROFESSOR PORTERFOY. *(Looking at papers)* Mr. Jameson was shot by the bounty hunter trying to protect the boys. He was put in prison to await trial but passed away two days later. Mrs. Jameson caught a fever nursing him in his cell and followed him shortly thereafter. The farm was sold to pay the fine and the children were sent to live with an aunt in Pennsylvania.

TY. But what about the slaves – Fast and Slow?

PROFESSOR PORTERFOY. I couldn't find any trace of them. I expect they got away since there was no mention of them ever being caught.

MAGGIE. What happened to Calico?

PROFESSOR PORTERFOY. I couldn't find anything about her, either. She must have gotten away into the woods and somehow made it up to Canada.

*(**TY** suddenly gets up and begins throwing books from the bookcase shelves.)*

MRS. WILLIAMS. Ty, what in the world… ?

TY. The secret cupboard! It's got to be behind this book-case!

PROFESSOR PORTERFOY. Oh, I doubt that. This place has probably been remodeled many times.

(*JANIE and MAGGIE help TY.*)

JANIE. I bet it hasn't! I bet it's still right back here! There's got to be a catch or...(*TY finds the catch.*) Wait! I think...

(*TY releases the catch and the bookcase door opens.*)

TY. Wow!

JANIE. It was here all the time!

(*EVERYONE is peering into the cupboard.*)

PROFESSOR PORTERFOY. Wait, don't go in there! This is a rare historic find! It mustn't be trampled. (*To MR. WIL-LIAMS*) Have you got a flashlight?

(*MR. WILLIAMS exits to kitchen.*)

PROFESSOR PORTERFOY. Extraordinary! I'm afraid you're going to have to stay in your hotel for a few more days. This place is about to be overrun by historians. Won't that be thrilling?

TY. (*Sarcastically*) Oh yeah, that won't suck out all the excite-ment or anything.

(*MR. WILLIAMS returns with a flashlight which he hands to PROFESSOR PORTERFOY who switches it on and enters the cupboard.*)

PROFESSOR PORTERFOY. Amazing! To think I'm the first person to step in here in 150 years...

(*PROFESSOR PORTERFOY re-enters carrying the Barbie doll.*)

PROFESSOR PORTERFOY. Does this belong to anyone?

MAGGIE. My Barbie! I knew you took her, Ty!

TY. I didn't! Honest, Mom...

PROFESSOR PORTERFOY. (*Back in the closet*) Oh, my good-ness! I think...I think I found your ghost! Ahhh!

(*A thump. Everyone gasps.*)

PROFESSOR PORTERFOY. It's all right – I tripped! I'm okay! Oh my goodness…Mr. Williams, come in and take a look at this, would you? Here, way in the back…is this what I think it is?

*(***MR. WILLIAMS*** *enters cupboard.)*

MRS. WILLIAMS. What is it?!

JANIE. What are you looking at?!

MR. WILLIAMS. *(Off)* We found her! I don't believe it! After all these years, we finally found her!

MRS. WILLIAMS. What?!

TY. Who?!

MR. WILLIAMS. *(Entering from cupboard holding the hair ribbon)* Calico! We found Calico! She never made it out to the woods after all.

PROFESSOR PORTERFOY. *(Entering)* There's a nasty wound in the skull. Poor thing probably got a concussion when that bounty hunter hit her. She crawled in here, shut the door, fell asleep and just never woke up.

JANIE. And nobody ever looked for her because they figured she'd gotten away. Oh, that's so sad.

PROFESSOR PORTERFOY. Amazing. To think she's been here all this time…

MAGGIE. No wonder she took my Barbie. She was scared of being alone.

TY. And that's why all that stuff has been happening! She wanted us to find her! She wanted us to rescue her!

JANIE. It wasn't the dead poisoned dog at all!

MR. WILLIAMS. So what do we do now?

PROFESSOR PORTERFOY. *(Shutting the secret door)* I suppose we call the police.

MAGGIE. But what'll happen to her?

PROFESSOR PORTERFOY. Calico? I suppose the county coroner will take the remains away and examine them.

JANIE. But she won't be happy then. She wants to finish riding the Railroad up north to Canada where she can be free with her Ma!

MR. WILLIAMS. Janie, we are not smuggling the bones of a slave child across the border into Canada to bury her.

MRS. WILLIAMS. That's exactly what we should do!

MR. WILLIAMS. Fine – that can be your first field trip when they let you out of the lunatic asylum.

MRS. WILLIAMS. Honey, think about it. It's what Calico wants.

MR. WILLIAMS. I hardly think Professor Porterfoy will go along with it. Tell her, Professor.

PROFESSOR PORTERFOY. Actually, I think they're right.

TY. We're going to Canada! I'm going to shoot a moose!

JANIE. I'm going to marry a Mountie!

MR. WILLIAMS. Wait a minute! *(To* **PROFESSOR PORTERFOY***)* What about the historical significance?

PROFESSOR PORTERFOY. What good will it do anybody to have some poor, little child's remains gone over with a fine tooth comb?

JANIE. See, Daddy? It's five against one.

MAGGIE. Six against one – don't forget Calico!

TY. We win!

MR. WILLIAMS. We can't just stick the bones in the trunk and drive over the border!

PROFESSOR PORTERFOY. Why not? We could hide them. And we're only going to do what the authorities will do eventually anyway.

JANIE. You're always talking about history coming alive, Daddy. Now it's alive right in front of your face and you're pooping out.

MAGGIE. She's *our* ghost. *We* should make it right.

JANIE. Let's go find something nice to put her in. I have my old baby blanket around somewhere…

MAGGIE. And she can take my Barbie with her. I don't mind.

TY. I can build her a special box…

(**JANIE**, **MAGGIE** *and TY exit to kitchen.*)

MR. WILLIAMS. *(Calling after them)* This is so not over!

MRS. WILLIAMS. If it helps you to think that way, dear. Professor, might I offer you a cup of coffee?

PROFESSOR PORTERFOY. That would be delightful. You wouldn't have a few biscuits laying around, would you?

(**MRS. WILLIAMS** *and* **PROFESSOR PORTERFOY** *exit to kitchen.*)

MR. WILLIAMS. Wait a minute! Wait a minute! I'm putting my foot down this time! I'll...I'll sick the dead, poisoned dog on you! You'll be sorry!

(**MR. WILLIAMS** *exits to kitchen. A pause. The room is the opposite of what we saw in the opening moments – it is now bright, warm, happy. The shadow has been lifted. Creaking, the bookcase cupboard door opens by itself. We hear "Follow The Drinking Gourd." There is the sound of a child's soft, happy laughter.*)

Curtain

COSTUMES

The costumes are pretty easy. no one has to change costumes, unless the williams family wants to change their shirts at some point to indicate time passing.

MR. WILLIAMS - pants and shirt
MRS. WILLIAMS - pants and shirt
MAGGIE - pants or shorts and shirt
TY - pants or shorts and shirt
JANIE - pants or shorts and shirt
SUZE - pants or shorts and shirt
BECKA - pants or shorts and shirt
MADAME ROSA - colorful skirt and blouse or dress, wispy
    shawl, lots of jewelry
PROFESSOR PORTERFOY - dress or skirt, blouse and a
    blazer
MR. JAMESON - period trousers and shirt, maybe a jacket
    and hat
MRS. JAMESON - period dress and apron
ELIJAH - period trousers and shirt
TEMPERANCE - period dress and apron
FAITH - period dress and apron
REVEREND MATTHEWS - period dark suit
CALICO - raggedy dress, no shoes
FAST - raggedy pants and shirt, no shoes
SLOW - raggedy pants and shirt, no shoes
MR. COLLINS - period rough pants, shirt, hat, jacket
SLATTERY - period rough pants, shirt, hat, jacket
COOMBS - period rough pants, shirt, hat, jacket

PROPS

curtains on window
sheets on furniture
boxes, bags, suitcases
books for bookcase
barbie doll
armful of logs
cup of coffee
"miss alice" wooden doll
2 rifles
ouija board
carrot
hollowed out "bible" containing pistol
wet cloth
hot brick
pitcher of lemonade & glasses on a tray
hair ribbon
carved wooden "charm"
briefcase containing papers
diary and pen & inkpot
dish of butter
false "slave receipts"
flashlight

Also by
Steph DeFerie

Nick Tickle, Fairy Tale Detective

Once Upon a Wolf

After the Rain King

Emmalina Scrooge

A Play About A Dragon

Return Of The King

Please consult the
Baker's Plays Catalogue
for complete details or find us online at
www.bakersplays.com